Golden Lion Tamarin Monkeys

Focus: Endangered Animals

Meredith Costain

Tamarins are small monkeys. They live in trees. Tamarins stay with their families until they are grown.

Baby tamarins are very small. They are small enough to fit into your hand! Until they can climb, baby tamarins ride on their parents' backs.

There are many kinds of tamarins. Each kind has special markings. This tamarin has white markings on its chest.

This is a golden lion
tamarin. It has golden fur.
It has a mane like a lion.
There are not many
golden lion tamarins
left in the world.

Golden lion tamarins live in rainforests in South America. But many rainforests have been cut down. People need to plant more rainforests. People need to save the rainforests. Then the golden lion tamarins will be safe.

Zoos are helping golden lion tamarins. Zoos have made places where they can live and be safe. People can see the golden lion tamarins in the trees. Then people will want to keep tamarins safe.

Sometimes, zoos put golden lion tamarins back in the rainforests. First they show the tamarins how to find food and stay safe. People want golden lion tamarins to live for a very long time.